For my mom and dad — J.K.
To Cat — R.W.

MISS TURIE'S MAGIC CREATURES

WRITTEN BY JOY KELLER

ILLUSTRATED BY RICHARD WATSON

Watch her fly and climb and wrestle.
How she loves to exercise! Would you like to pick her up?
I don't think that's very wise.

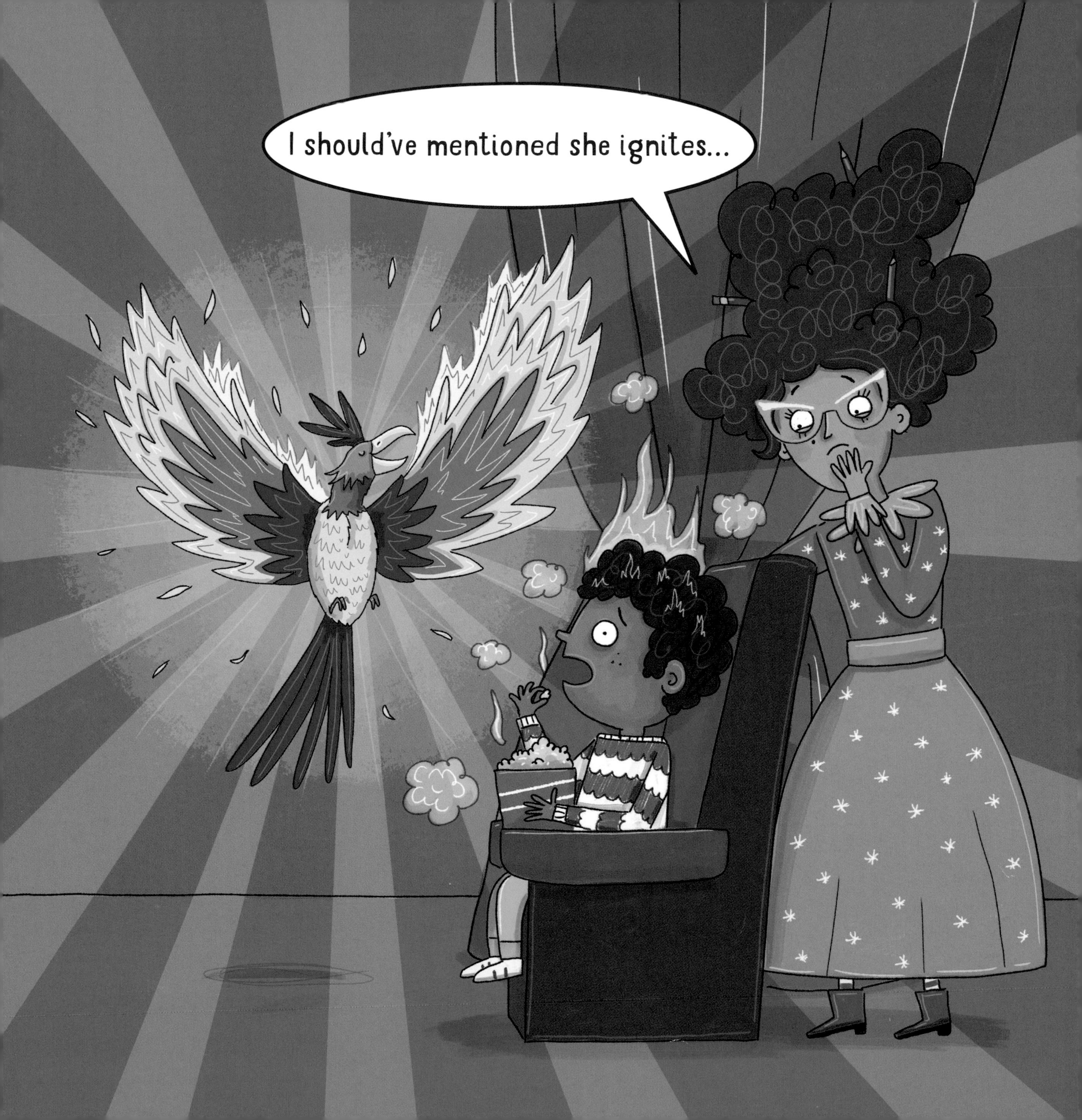
I should've mentioned she ignites...

Unicorn (Europe)

Medieval Europeans believed that unicorn horns could be ground up to make medicines or dipped in drinks to detect poison. The horns were more valuable than gold, and Queen Elizabeth I had a unicorn horn among her crown jewels. So where did all these unicorn horns come from? They were most likely rhinoceros horns or the tusks of toothed whales called narwhals.

Dragon (Europe and Asia)

Dragons appear in stories from across the globe. In European legends, dragons were dangerous creatures that hoarded treasure. In Asia, however, dragons were thought to be powerful and kind. They could breathe clouds, make rain, and change the seasons.

Hydra (Greece)

The Hydra was a many-headed, serpent-like monster. In one Greek legend, the hero Hercules defeated the nine-headed Lernaean Hydra, a creature so fierce it grew back two heads for every one Hercules cut off.

Hippocamp (Phoenicia and Greece)

The hippocamp (or hippocampus) was a sea horse. The Greeks believed that the sea god Poseidon rode in a chariot pulled by a team of hippocampi.

Phoenix (Egypt)

Legend says the firebird could live for hundreds of years, but only one could exist at a time. This lone phoenix eventually flew to the Temple of the Sun to make a nest of cinnamon twigs. After the sun set the nest on fire, a new phoenix rose from the ashes.

Pegasus (Greece)

Pegasus was the famous winged horse of Greek mythology. He carried thunder and lightning for Zeus, the king of the gods.

Cerberus (Greece)

This three-headed dog was also known as the "Hound of Hades" because he guarded the gates of the underworld. He let the dead in…and made sure nobody got out.

Griffin (North Africa, Middle East, and Europe)

Tales of the griffin date back to 3300 BC. These stories were probably told to explain the strange fossils found by ancient miners in the Gobi Desert. Scientists now know these fossils belonged to a dinosaur called Protoceratops.

Kraken (Scandinavia)

Scandinavian sailors told tales of a giant squid that lurked deep in the waters off the coast of Norway. The kraken was so large—over a mile around—that it created a whirlpool when it submerged.

Loch Ness Monster (Scotland)

For decades, people have tried to prove that a sea monster lives in Loch Ness in the Scottish Highlands. The most famous photograph of the Loch Ness Monster was taken by a London surgeon in 1934, but it turned out to be a hoax. The "monster" was made from a toy submarine.

Sasquatch (North America)

Sasquatch (or Bigfoot) is said to be a huge, ape-like creature that lives in the woods of North America. Scientists believe that Sasquatch is a hoax, but many people continue to search for evidence of its existence.

Golem (Eastern Europe)

In Jewish folklore, a golem was a clay monster brought to life to serve its master. Those creating a golem needed to be careful; golems often became too powerful for their masters to control.

Chimera (Greece)

This dangerous, fire-breathing monster was a strange mixture of several creatures. It was most commonly described as having the head of a lion, the body of a goat, and the tail of a snake.

Cat (Everywhere!)

Ancient people all over the world knew that cats were special—almost magical—creatures. Cats hunted pests that damaged food supplies and carried dangerous diseases, so they were important to human survival. It's no wonder cats were often connected to gods and goddesses in mythology! Here is a look at cats in the ancient world:

The Vikings believed that the goddess Freya rode in a chariot pulled by cats, and many Vikings kept cats in their homes and on their ships for good luck.

In ancient Egypt, people worshipped several cat goddesses. Egyptian cat owners treated their cats like family members, and hurting a cat was considered a serious crime.

A common symbol in Japan is the *maneki neko*, an image of a cat with one raised paw. According to legend, this cat once saved the life of an emperor by beckoning him away from danger. The *maneki neko* is thought to bring good luck when given as a gift.

LCCN 2018942423
ISBN 9781943147410

Text copyright © 2018 by Joy Keller
Illustrations by Richard Watson
Illustrations copyright © 2018 by The Innovation Press

Published by The Innovation Press
1001 4th Avenue, Suite 3200, Seattle, WA 98154
www.theinnovationpress.com

Printed and bound by Worzalla
Production date May 2018

Cover lettering by Nicole LaRue
Cover art by Richard Watson
Book layout by Tim Martyn